The Clothesline

by
Orbie

Owlkids Books

To Réal, who inspired this story (thank you!),
and to all the kids who have found
themselves stuck on a clothesline —O.

My name is Reggie.

I'm five years old.

I live here, above the corner store.

It's handy because when I get my allowance,
I don't have to go far to buy treats.

Mom gives me an allowance for doing chores around the house.

She calls me her big helper, and she gives me her change.

I zip down the stairs really fast. Just like a superhero.

But not if Mom is watching because it would scare her.

tap
tap
tap
tap

On the way down, I like to give the knot in the clothesline a good yank.

tap
tap
tap

I can't help it.

I love the sound it makes.

This morning, I helped Mom pick up my toys AND I vacuumed.

I like helping Mom.

She must have been happy with my work
because she gave me thirty cents!

Three dimes!

Thirty cents!!!

I was excited about all
the candy I could buy.

I ran down the stairs
even faster than usual.

Maybe too fast . . .

because I lost my footing . . .

just as I grabbed onto
the knot in the clothesline.

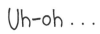

My name is Reggie.

I'm five years old.

And I'm stuck in the
middle of a clothesline.

or I help my left hand with my right.

But then I'd have to drop my three dimes.

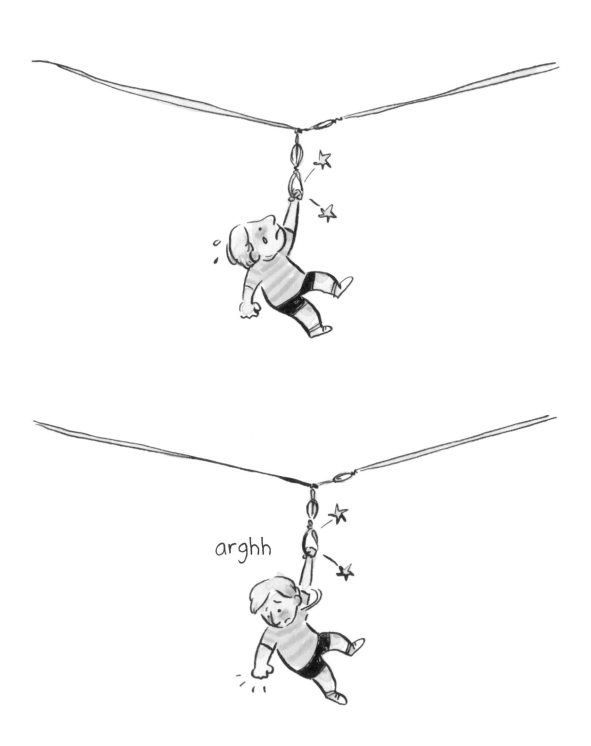

I decide to try holding on with both hands, WITHOUT letting go of my money.

That doesn't work.

clink

clink

clink

So I shout for help, as
LOUD as I can.

As loud as I'm scared.

As loud as I'm mad that I dropped
my thirty cents.

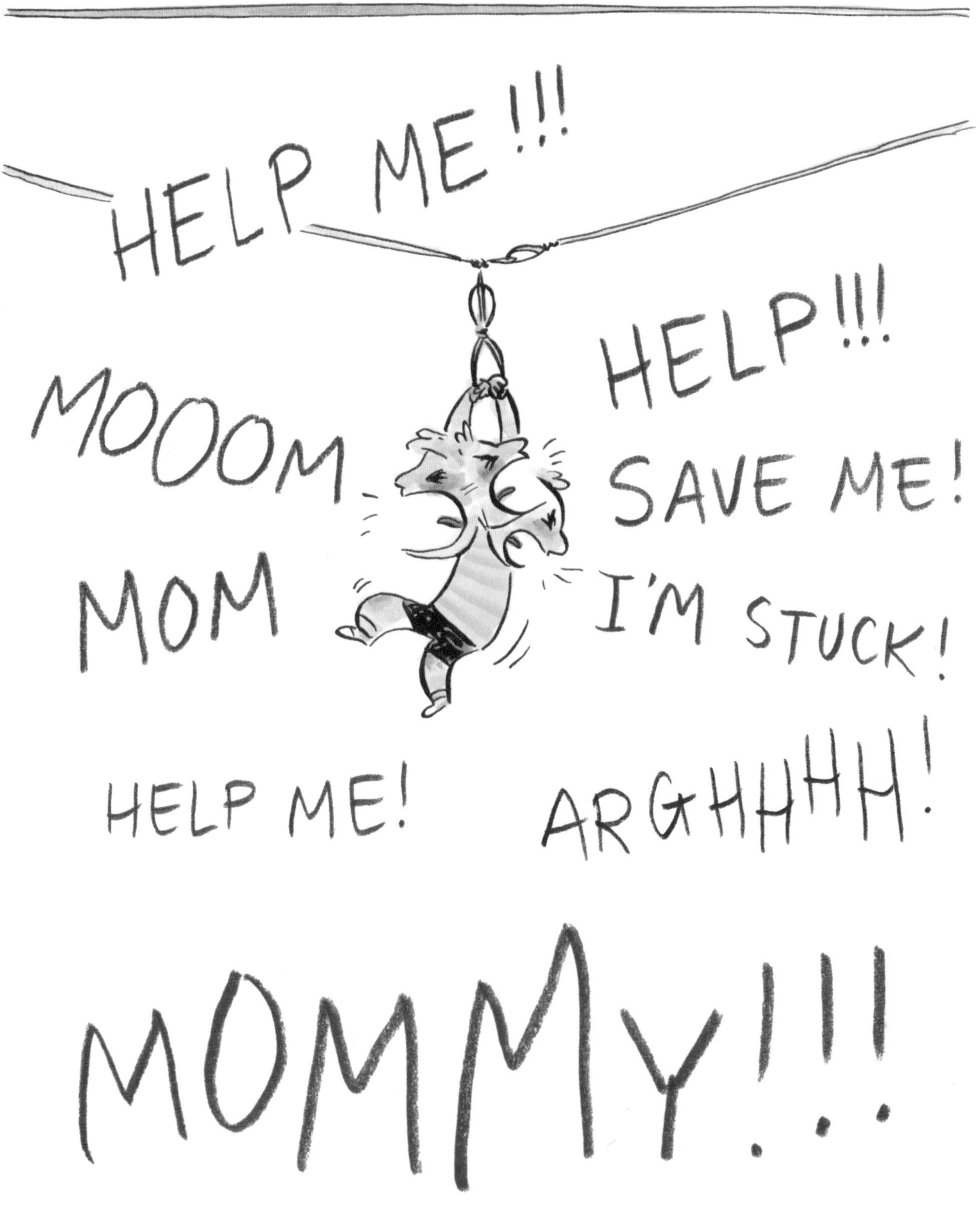
HELP ME!!!
MOOOM
HELP!!!
SAVE ME!
MOM
I'M STUCK!
HELP ME!
ARGHHHH!
MOMMY!!!

Mom . . .

But nobody
hears me.

Not even my mom, who
can usually hear mischief
from a mile away.

What do I do now?

I don't cry.

At least not very much . . .

Oooh . . .

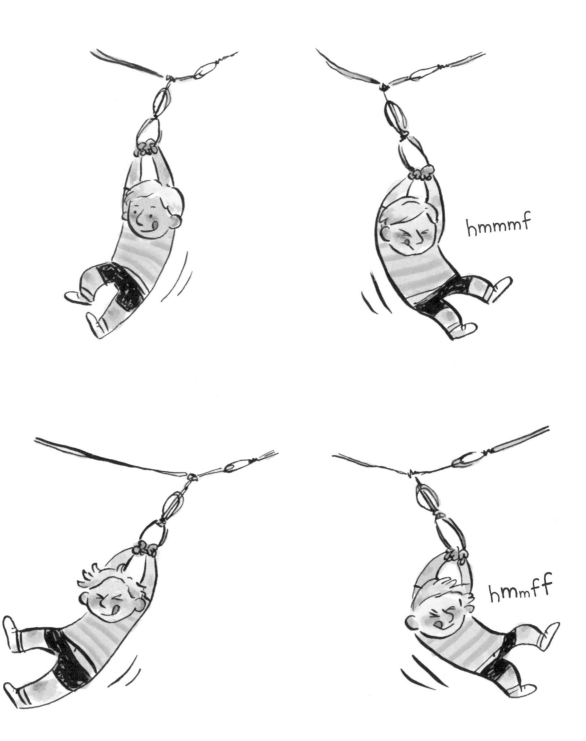

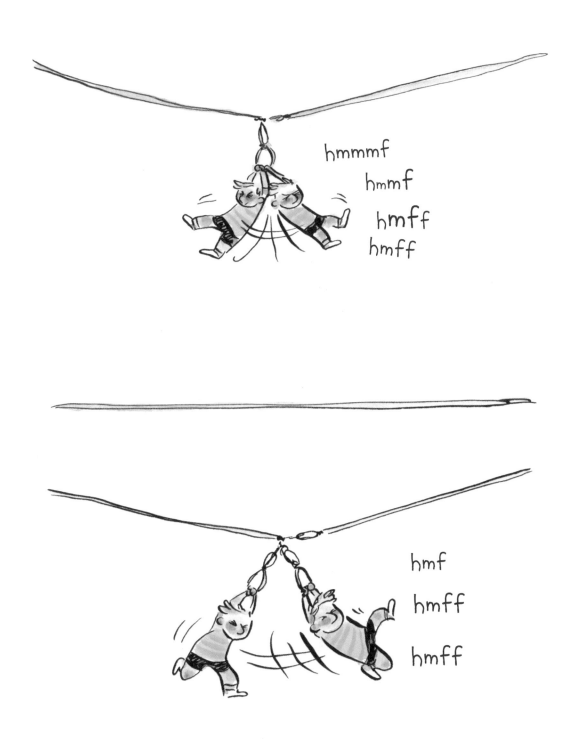

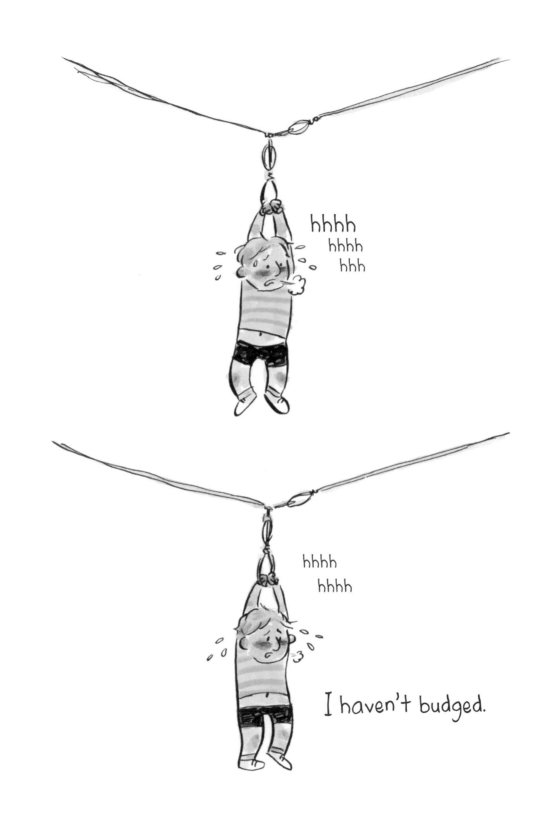

So I wait.

Wait for someone to walk by.

For someone to see me.

For someone to save me.

But nobody comes.

Well, almost nobody . . .

You're probably wondering what I'm doing up here?

I'm asking myself the same question.

My hands hurt . . .

ouch

I'm scared of plunging to my death.

ouch

There are usually people walking by.

Where are they now?

It's been a long time.

The only way to get down,

. . . is to let go of the knot.

I don't have a choice . . .

gulp!

In five . . .

Four . . .

Three . . .

Two . . .

One . . .

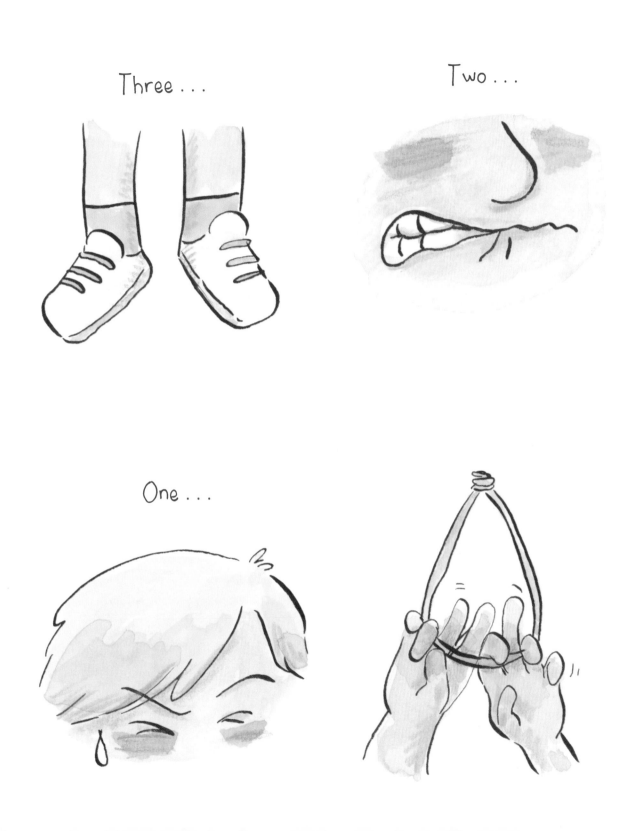

At some point she'll notice I haven't come back.

It's been a really long time since I left.

Ow . . .

It's over . . .

ding
ding ♫

The next week . . .

My name is Reggie.

I'm five years old.

When I go down the stairs now,

I look at the knot in the clothesline,

but I DON'T TOUCH IT!